O'Brien P ...o
From: ...nagement
To: ...mbers of Staff
Subject: The Forbidden Files

You're probably wondering why you arrived this morning to find the police searching your desks.

The safe containing the Forbidden Files was broken into. The Files have been STOLEN.

The stories in these Files were kept locked up and hidden away for good reason. These stories are too FRIGHTENING, too DISTURBING or just too downright DISGUSTING to be read by children.

The police will want to speak to all of you — please give them your full cooperation. We have to find The Forbidden Files; they must NEVER see the light of day.

TOO LATE, SUCKERS!

Have You Seen
This Man?

OISÍN McGANN grew up in the suburban backstreets of Dublin and Drogheda. He has never had a **proper job**, but he has written and illustrated numerous children's books of **questionable quality**. McGann is known as a **loner** with few friends. If you should see this man, **do not approach him,** as he may be **rude**.

THE POISON FACTORY

Written and illustrated by

Oisín McGann

THE O'BRIEN PRESS
DUBLIN

First published 2006 by The O'Brien Press Ltd,
12 Terenure Road East, Rathgar, Dublin 6, Ireland
Tel: +353 1 4923333; Fax: +353 1 4922777
E-mail: books@obrien.ie
Website: www.obrien.ie
Reprinted 2007.

ISBN: 978-0-86278-941-1

British Library Cataloguing-in-Publication Data
McGann, Oisin
The poison factory. - (Forbidden Files)
1. Horror tales 2. Children's Stories
I. Title
823.9'2[J]

2 3 4 5 6 7 8 9

07 08 09 10

The O'Brien Press receives assistance from

Layout and design: The O'Brien Press
Printed and bound in the UK by J.H. Haynes & Co Ltd, Sparkford

CONTENTS

1 Going Under The Wall   7

2 The Hunt For Molars   16

3 Dead On Their Feet   25

4 Total Loss Of Control   34

5 The Disgustinger   42

6 The Kitchen Of Death   55

7 Dying To Go   72

For the lads in the M&M studio, back in the day.
Thanks for all the laughs.

1

Going Under The Wall

They called it 'The Fart Factory', it smelled so bad. The Kanker & Byle Chemical Company was a towering heap of buildings and pipes and walkways, just piled on top of each other. Then somebody had stuck some chimneys on the top, like candles on the world's ugliest birthday cake. Gluey smoke rose out of the chimneys, but then fell over the sides and poured to the ground, too oily and lazy to float up into the sky.

And it was a spooky place too. Apart from the delivery trucks that only showed up late at night, nobody was ever seen going in, or coming out. Nobody knew anybody who had ever been inside. Some people said the place was haunted, that it was run by ghosts and ghouls.

Or maybe robots.

There was only one piece of grass in the area, and it lay right next to the factory wall. Like most things near the factory, the grass was brown, and slightly greasy, but it was still better than the tarmac of the road for playing football. And you were less likely to get hit by a car. So this was where Gaz Flynn and the other members of the Root Street Gang played soccer.

It started out like a normal Saturday – Gaz, Joey, Damo and Hayley had gone out to the brown to play football. Gaz and Damo were always the captains of their teams, because Joey (Gaz's baby brother) was only seven, and couldn't kick a ball to save his life, and Hayley was, well … a *girl*.

It stopped being a normal Saturday when Joey took careful aim at the goal painted onto the wall of the factory and kicked the ball as hard as he could, sending it soaring into the air and over the factory wall.

'You maggot!' Gaz snapped at his little brother, grabbing him by his mop of thick, black hair. 'That's the third time you've done that.'

'It was an accident!' Joey snapped back, pulling himself free.

'It's *always* an accident with you, you little twerp,' Gaz shouted at him, his brown face going a strange purple colour. 'This is the last time. You're going in there and getting that ball!'

The others gaped at him in shock.

'You can't send him in there, man,' Damo gasped, in his best American accent. 'Not into the *factory*. That's way too cruel.'

Damo always tried to act like he was some US rap star (even though he was from Root Street like the rest of them) but he'd never even been to America. He wore his baseball cap crooked all the time and made strange shapes with his hands while he talked. He also wished he had African blood in him, like Gaz and Joey, but he was as white as vanilla ice cream and had red hair.

'I've had enough of him,' Gaz declared. 'That's the third ball he's lost in there.'

He turned to his brother.

'That's it. If you ever want to play with us again, you're going in to get that ball.'

Joey looked as if he was going to cry, but Gaz folded his arms and put on his grimmest expression. They were very alike, Gaz and Joey. With their brown freckled skin, their black hair and the same stubborn look on their faces, you could tell they were brothers. But Gaz was bigger, and he had an earring, and lines shaved into the sides of his head that made him look even meaner than he was. And he was feeling pretty mean right then. Joey looked out from under his ropey fringe of hair at Hayley, who was normally nicer to him than the two older boys. He gave her his best baby-eyes look, but she just shrugged.

'It'll be okay. I can tell,' she tried to reassure him. 'I know you'll find that ball, no problem.'

Hayley thought that she was a bit psychic. Nobody else did.

'It's only a factory,' she added, one hand nervously twisting her curly, sand-coloured locks.

But it wasn't just any factory. It was Kanker & Byle.

There had once been guard dogs in the yard behind that wall – rottweilers and german shepherds, the meanest you'd ever seen. The only thing was, a dog has a sense of smell that's a thousand times better than a human's. There was a hole under

the mossy, grey concrete wall around the back of the factory, where the guard dogs – in a desperate bid to escape the stink – had dug their way out and run howling down the street, never to be seen again.

This was where Joey would have to go in. The Root Street Gang made their way round to the back wall, where they found the hole, hidden by a half-dead clump of thistles.

'Right, in you go,' Gaz told him. 'And don't mess about. Your mission is to just grab the ball and come back. I'm timing you. And don't make any noise. And if anybody catches you, don't tell them about us. Nobody likes a squealer. Now, go on.'

Joey looked around wide-eyed at the other two,

still hoping that one of them would stick up for him. But Gaz was the leader of the gang, and nobody argued with him when his lips went all thin like that. He could get really worked up when things didn't go his way. Joey got down on his knees, trying to push the stalks of the thistles aside, but the prickly plants still snagged on his clothes as he crawled down into the hole. The wall was a metre thick, and he had to pull himself along on his elbows to get up to the other side. Gaz's eyes followed his little brother's

feet as they disappeared, and then they all knelt down to watch Joey go through.

'You'll be right as rain!' Hayley whispered, just before she lost sight of him.

They all sat back on the ground, eyes fixed on the hole, and waited for Joey to return. And they waited. And they waited. And they kept waiting.

Suddenly, the sound of a scream made them jump to their feet. It was Joey – there was no mistaking his voice. He screamed like he was seeing something that was scaring him out of his mind. Then he shrieked again, as if he was fighting for his life. Then he gave another, weaker scream; a horrible, final, despairing cry that was cut off abruptly, leaving an eerie silence. Gaz, Hayley and Damo stood, clutching one another and trembling.

'He could be having us on,' Gaz said. 'He's just messing us about.'

'That sounded real to me,' Hayley whimpered, close to tears.

'And his aura is in pain, I can feel it!'

'I don't know about his aura, but he's good at screaming,' Gaz told her. 'He's always screaming.'

'Yeah, but, like normally you're the one *making* him scream, man,' Damo said softly, pointing at Gaz with both hands like a gangsta rapper. 'He was all on his own in there. And that didn't sound like he was trying to get you in trouble with your momma. That sounded like … like …' He didn't want to say what they were all thinking.

Gaz gazed down at the hole in the ground, anger boiling up inside him. Trust Joey to get in trouble. If he went home without his little brother, their mother would have a fit. And Gaz was bound to get the blame. He let out a yell and kicked the wall a few times until he was able to calm down a bit.

'Right,' he said, breathing deeply as he stared down at the hole. 'S'ppose we'd better go and get him then.'

2

The Hunt For Molars

The smell was thicker on the other side of the wall. Gaz was always the first one in the gang to take risks – he was more afraid of being seen as a chicken than getting hurt. He led the way under the wall, squeezing through the small hole, dragging himself under and finally pulling himself out the other side, carefully brushing the dirt from his beloved trainers.

The air had a chemical feel to it; it felt damp against his face, and he could feel the stink soaking into his skin and his clothes. Damo crawled out behind him, nodding his head like he was listening to music, as he did whenever he was nervous. Then Hayley appeared, chewing on her fingernails as she looked around. The pink blotches on her cheeks always got bigger when she was scared. Now they were covering most of her face. They all stood and stared.

There were wooden crates and stacks of barrels and plastic containers on pallets, lines and lines of them stretching out before them.

'How are we going to find the little guy in here?' Damo groaned softly, his hands waving in front of him. 'This is freaking me out. I think we should get out of here, and call in the cops.'

'They'd never believe us. They know what we're like,' Gaz replied. 'We're going to have to find him ourselves. We're going to get him out of here, and then I'm going to give him a right kick up the bum for scaring us. Now, come on.'

They walked past the stacks of containers until they came to the wall of a building. The sound of an engine made them duck behind a pile of metal barrels, and a forklift drove past. It had driven out of a large door off to one side. Gaz waved at the others to follow him, and they crept inside the building.

There were more pallets inside, with thousands of small bottles and packages stacked up and bound with plastic sheeting.

'Hey guys!' Damo whispered. 'Check it out! There's pirates here!'

He was pointing at a label that had a skull-and-crossbones on it. Hayley thumped his arm.

'That's the sign for *poison*, you turnip!' she sneered. 'Don't you know anything?'

'They've all got that label,' Gaz said. 'Everything in here's poisonous. I wonder what it is?'

'Oh, all sorts of useful things,' a voice said from behind them.

They all spun round, and then froze. Standing right there, right in

front of them, was a tall, spindly man with a sticking-out belly, large, bony hands and feet, and a face that looked like it had never seen a good night's sleep. Dressed in a white coat, he was smiling, showing teeth that barely clung to his gums.

'It's alright, there's no need to be afraid,' he reassured them. 'I just work here, I'm nobody. My name's Cornelius. Welcome to the factory! Are you here to inquire about our poisons?'

'We're looking for–' Gaz began.

'We have whatever you need!' Cornelius cut him off. 'And this year our range is bigger and more exciting than ever! Our customers come from all over the world, and from every walk of life. From secret agents to evil queens; from wicked witches to sinister sorcerors …'

'We're trying to–' Gaz tried to interrupt.

'… from alien invaders to desperate babysitters; from pygmies to politicians, gangsters to grandmothers, mad scientists to– eh?'

He stopped short when Gaz poked him in the belly.

'We're looking for my little brother,' Gaz said, folding his arms and sticking his chin out to hide his nervousness. 'He came in here a few minutes ago, and then we heard him screaming. Now he's gone missing. If you know where he is, you'd better tell us, right?'

The man lifted one hand to tap a long fingernail against his teeth. The teeth rattled with each tap.

'Screaming, you say? Hmmmm. Missing?', he muttered, looking more and more worried as he tapped. 'Hmmmmmm. Not good. Not good at all.'

He threw a fearful glance towards the dark shadows of the warehouse. Then he bent down and spoke to the children in a careful whisper.

'It sounds as if your young friend has fallen into the hands of our Head Of Security, Molars. An ogre of a man; over-large and ever-so-slightly monstrous. I'm sure he wouldn't hurt your young friend, but his appearance alone can be a cause for alarm. It's the extra eye, you understand, and the nose covered in warts. And the teeth sticking out of his chin … *I* sometimes feel like screaming when I look at him – and I've known him for years.'

'What … what do we do?' Hayley asked, her teeth gnawing away at the last of her thumbnail. 'How do we get Joey back?'

'You'll need to bribe Molars,' the man told them. 'He's a terror for kidnapping people, but he's got a real sweet tooth. Now, let me see here …'

He fumbled around inside his coat, searching for something.

'Ah! Here we are!'

Pulling a bag from his pocket, he held it out to the children.

'I was keeping these sweets for my break, but you can have them. I'm trying to cut down anyway. Just give him these, and I'm sure he'll let your friend go.'

Cornelius leaned in closer.

'And if you want to take one or two for yourselves … well, who's going to know? Just make sure you leave plenty for him. There you are now. He'll be on the top floor, in the security office. Run along now, I won't tell a soul that I've seen you. Good luck!'

Gaz looked at the bag Cornelius had given him with some suspicion. But the man pushed him gently towards the stairs at the back of the warehouse.

'Hurry!' he urged them. 'Before somebody comes! You can bribe Molars, but you don't want to run into the boss, or those cooks! Then you'd be in real trouble. Hurry, now!'

Clutching the bag, Gaz nodded to the other two, and they took off at a run, being careful to keep behind the piles of boxes until they reached the stairs. At the top of the steps, there was a door, standing ajar. Gazing up at the door, the remaining three members of the Root Street Gang hesitated, frightened of what lay beyond it.

'For Joey,' Gaz said softly.

'For Joey,' the other two repeated, nodding.

Creeping up the stairs, they pushed through the door, and into the dimly-lit corridor beyond. There came the sound of machinery, and the insect-like buzz of a hundred voices. The only other door in the corridor was at the end – and it led out into a room full of people. And something about those

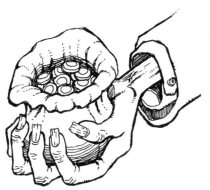

voices did not sound right.

3

Dead On Their Feet

The three children tiptoed to the end of the corridor and peered round the door. They were looking down on a factory floor; what looked like a packing plant. Bottles of all shapes and sizes travelled through the plant on conveyor belts, and were being packed up in boxes, which were then carried by more conveyors out through wide hatches at the far end of the huge room. It would all have been fairly normal, if not for the zombies.

'Holy Moses–' Damo blurted out, before Hayley clapped a hand over his mouth.

They had to be zombies, the living dead – there was no way they were still alive, with their flesh all rotting like that, bits of bone sticking out, and expressions on their faces like they'd drunk too

much seawater. They walked with arms stretched out in front of them, and they talked constantly. Mostly, they just repeated words like 'Food', or 'Meat', or even just 'Grarrr'. They all wore overalls, and each zombie had a name badge.

There were dozens of them, all in different stages of rotting. They were working along the conveyor belts, packing pills, capsules and liquids into the bottles. The decomposing workers at the ends of the belts shovelled the bottles into boxes. They all looked as if they were in a bad mood, and most of them had hungry expressions on their faces.

There was a different smell in this part of the factory; a stale, vinegary odour, as if all the zombies had been pickled. The Root Street Gang looked down on them in horror.

'How do we get past the dead dudes?' Damo whined. 'There's no way!'

'Ssh!' Gaz hushed him. 'Look, there's a door over there. That must be the way through. If we can get down the stairs, we can sneak along under that conveyor belt there and get out that way.'

The other two looked to where he was pointing, and then stared at him as if he was mad. But it appeared to be the only way, and neither of them wanted to leave Joey trapped in this horrible place. There was nothing for it but to take the chance.

Gaz put a hand on each of their shoulders and gave them a grim nod, like he had seen the commanders do in war films. Then he waited until all of the zombies were looking away and darted down the metal steps and across to the conveyor belt by the wall. Once she was sure he'd made it, Hayley followed, almost tripping near the bottom of the steps. Her pink-blotched cheeks glowing like a traffic light, she ran across and slid in behind Gaz. Damo skidded in beside them a moment later.

'Right,' Gaz panted. 'I think ... eh, let's go, then.'

The conveyor belt rattled over their heads as they crawled quickly along the floor. A zombie lurched past them and something suddenly dropped onto the floor and bounced under the belt – right beside

Hayley. It was a half-rotten ear. She jammed her mouth into Gaz's back to muffle her scream, and grabbed hold of his leg so tightly he nearly let out a yelp. It was a good thing she had hardly any fingernails. The zombie grunted and bent down, fumbling around in the shadows under the belt. Hayley's grip on Gaz's calf muscle tightened and he winced at the pain. The zombie's clawing hand came closer to her knees. She shuffled back as far as she could

go, but they were right up against the wall. The hand was inches from her.

Gaz reached back with the toe of his trainer and pushed the zombie's ear into the path of its searching fingers. The hand came upon the missing body part and grabbed at it. There was a moan of relief, the arm disappeared, and the zombie continued on its way.

'I think I'm going to be sick,' Hayley gulped.

'You can't,' Gaz told her. 'They'll hear you.'

She decided she'd be all right after all. They crawled on, reaching the door on the other side of the factory room. In a frantic dash, they sprinted through the open door. Jets of gas hit them as they rushed in and they had to hold their noses as they stumbled through a tiled room filled with clouds of steam and into the corridor beyond. They were in a long, narrow hallway with big lockers against the walls. Their skin and clothes were damp from the gas, which smelled like disinfectant.

'S'like the stuff Momma uses to clean the toilet,'

Damo sniffed. 'Suppose with all the zombies rotting like that, there must be loads of germs around.'

'Well, I think it's stained my trainers,' Gaz complained. 'Mam'll kill me. These were almost brand new. I was at her for weeks to buy them!'

Hayley bent down and picked something up off a bench by the side of the lockers. It was a remote control for a television.

'What's that doing here?' Damo asked.

She didn't have time to reply. A siren was going off out on the factory floor. Staggering through the clouds of disinfectant steam was a huge, groaning zombie. The three children froze. There was nowhere to run. They would never make it to the other end of the corridor before it saw them. Gaz did the only thing he could; there was an open locker right next to him, and he jumped into it. No sooner was he inside, than Damo and Hayley piled in beside him. They pulled the door over just as the undead creature lurched out of the clouds of gas. They cowered in the tight space, watching through the slits in the metal door as it waddled down the corridor, followed by a second lumbering figure and then another.

'Must be break-time,' Gaz muttered.

One by one, all the zombies trudged past. None of them were coming near the lockers. There was nothing for the Root Street Gang to do but stay in hiding and wait.

4

Total Loss Of Control

S quashed into the locker, Gaz shivered as he thought about his brother. What if Molars was a zombie? Didn't zombies eat people? They did in all the horror films he wasn't supposed to watch.

Joey was a pain in the bum, but he didn't deserve to become zombie food.

Thinking of food, Gaz felt the bulge of the bag of sweets in his pocket. Jammed in the closed metal space of the locker, he could smell them too. He pulled them out. The smell was sweet and tingly. Almost irresistible. Cornelius had said they could take some – there were plenty in the bag. Gaz knew he shouldn't ... there were loads of reasons why he shouldn't ...

Opening the bag, he peeked inside. They were jellies. He loved jellies. He took one out, just to look at it. He'd put it right back. He smelled it; it smelled nice, like apple. It almost made him dizzy, it looked and smelled so good. It was in his mouth before he even knew it, almost as if his hand had a mind of its own. Chewing on it, he shrugged, savouring the taste. Damo was staring at the bag, which was being held up right in front of his face. Gaz handed it to him.

'Just take one,' he whispered, around the sweet between his teeth.

Damo picked out a black one, and popped it in his mouth.

'Dey're goodge,' he mumbled, still trying to use his hand to talk, and nearly sticking a finger in Gaz's eye.

Outside, the zombies continued to stagger past.

Damo offered the bag to Hayley. 'Have one.'

'No,' Hayley hissed. 'I've a funny feeling about those sweets. They're giving off a ... a negative energy.'

'What a load of rubbish. Take one!' Damo insisted.

'Yeah, go on,' Gaz repeated.

He was feeling a little guilty about taking one now that she'd said no. If she had one, he'd feel better about it.

'Mam told me never to take sweets from strangers,' Hayley told them, giving the bag a longing look. They did smell good.

'So what? *I'm* not a stranger,' Damo pointed out.

'Oh, yeah,' Hayley frowned, as she twisted the logic round in her head. 'I suppose that's alright then.'

She reached into the bag, and took an orange jelly.

'They're really nice,' she smiled, as she chewed. 'Sort of fizzy.'

Munching on their jellies, they waited for the zombies to go away.

'This is totally mental,' Damo muttered. 'What kind of factory uses zombies to pack boxes?'

'I don't want to find out,' Gaz said softly. 'That's the last of them. Let's get a move on.'

Very, very carefully, he opened the locker door and looked out. The corridor was empty. The three children tugged themselves free of the cramped space and nearly fell out into the hallway. There was only one way to go; a door at the very end of the corridor. But that was where the zombies had gone. They crept forward, none of them wanting to be first to look through the door. There was a low, angry groaning, and the sound of dozens of feet shuffling hurriedly around. The children's curiosity got the better of them. They all peeked their heads round the doorframe.

The door opened into a large lounge. It was filled with couches and armchairs, and a big wide-screen television hung on one wall. The living dead were milling around and moaning angrily. They were pulling up all the cushions on the couches, and turning over the furniture. They seemed very annoyed.

Hayley suddenly let rip with a loud belch, and Gaz and Damo turned to look at her in shock. One of the zombies – a woman with no nose and her teeth showing through her cheek – spun round and spotted the children. She stared for a moment, and then let out a hoarse bellow. The Root Street Gang screamed. The other zombies turned, and with a chorus of growls and snarls, staggered towards the children.

'LEG IT!' Gaz yelled.

And they did. They tore back the way they had come, through the gas-jet door, out onto the factory floor, with the zombies chasing them at a frightening speed for creatures that could only move at a lurch. As they passed one of the machines, Damo caught the hood of his tracksuit top on part of a conveyor belt. It lifted him off his feet, and dragged him up towards a hatch in the wall.

'Help!' he shouted, his would-be American accent lost in the panic. 'Oh, Holy God!'

The other two skidded to a halt, and turned just in time to see their friend disappear through the hatch. They stood stock-still for a moment, terrified by the sight of the zombies, but unable to leave Damo to his fate.

'Not him as well!' Gaz said through gritted teeth, realising how scared he was, and getting angry about it. 'I can't take my eyes off any of you for a *minute*. Right, come on!'

He sprinted back, and Hayley was forced to follow as he climbed onto the conveyor belt. As she grabbed on, Hayley realised she was still holding the remote control she had picked up. She threw it at the zombies with all her might. One of them caught it with surprising skill, and the others immediately turned on him and started pushing him around. A mumbling, moaning argument ensued, and Gaz and Hayley watched in relief as the conveyor belt carried them upwards.

'They just wanted their remote control,' Hayley said, in a sympathetic voice. 'Look, the poor things. All they wanted to do was watch telly.'

'I hate it when somebody else has the remote,'

Gaz nodded.

The conveyor belt trundled up and through the hatch, and they found themselves suddenly shrouded in darkness.

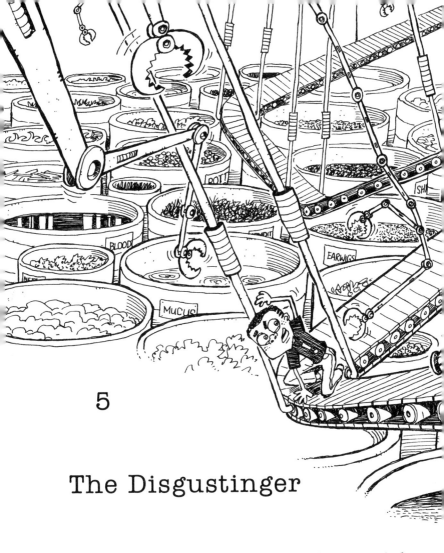

5

The Disgustinger

The conveyor belt picked up speed as it carried them through a dark, square tunnel. Up ahead, they could see Damo pulling his hood free of the steel pegs. Gaz and Hayley hung on to the

edges of the belt as they crawled forward to catch up with him. No sooner had they reached him, when the belt tilted and turned and they shrieked as they were thrown off, tumbling onto a second conveyor and clinging onto it for dear life as it clattered through another room, speeding them high above rows of bronze-coloured vats.

There were signs over the huge tanks, but Gaz was not sure he believed what he was reading. They whipped past below him; 'Jellied Slugs' said one; 'Used Earwax' said another. The belt dipped like a roller-coaster and he ducked under a third sign that read 'Dog's Drool', and yet another that said 'Armpit Hair'. All of the vats were full of the most disgusting things he'd ever heard of. There must have been tons of the stuff.

Suddenly, a row of robotic claws came dangling down from the ceiling, snapping at them, trying to drag the kids into the tanks.

'Aaagh!' Damo shouted. 'What's going on?'

'I think they're trying to sort us!' Gaz yelled back

as he dodged the grip of a steel claw. 'All that rubbish must get carried along here and dumped in those tanks!'

Damo went a yellowy-green colour and flattened himself against the belt to avoid a grasping robot hand. Hayley yelped as a claw managed to grab a tuft of her hair, and dropped it into one of the tanks.

'Hang on!' Gaz called to them. 'I think we're going to–'

The conveyor came to an abrupt end, and they fell screaming off the belt, down a chute and into a steel tank. Scrambling through a mass of white pellets to the edge of the metal box, Gaz saw that the whole thing was full of reject pills. He could tell they were rejects, because nobody can swallow something that's shaped like a star, or has hairs sticking out of it.

The other two crawled up beside him, trembling and breathless. One after another, they let out loud burps. Gaz felt gas rising in his throat, and then he

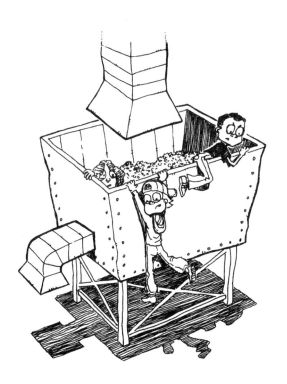

too gave a deep belch. They all looked at each other with puzzled expressions.

'What's the story here?' Damo wheezed, fixing his cap tighter onto his head. 'What was all that stuff for? This place is a nuthouse! And now we're completely lost. I WANNA GO HOME!'

'Shush!' Hayley said in an ominous voice, while rubbing her temples. 'I sense a great evil in this factory. This place has a very sickly aura.'

'That'll be the jellied slugs and the earwax,' Gaz snorted. 'Hey, maybe they feed that stuff to the zombies.'

Hayley screwed up her face.

'Nobody's *that* dead, Gaz.'

The three children climbed over the side of the container and dropped down to the floor. The room they were in was dark, but there was the light outline of a door only a few feet away.

'We're wasting time here anyway,' Gaz turned towards the door. 'Joey could be hurt or ... or worse. Come on, we haven't got all day.'

Damo threw a glance at Hayley, who rolled her eyes. Gaz could be a right pain when he tried to act the boss. Through the door was a flight of stairs, and at the top of the steps was the kind of corridor you'd find in a rich person's house, with gold-striped wallpaper and thick red carpet. There were paintings on the walls, the kind that didn't look like anything and strains of classical music could be heard from a door halfway down the corridor.

They were completely lost now, and they knew it. They had no choice but to check every room they came to, and hope that they might find some trace of Joey. But the Kanker & Byle factory was enormous, and now they couldn't even find their way out. And soon their mothers would start wondering where they were. Their footsteps were completely silent on the carpet, so they crept forward and peered in the door.

A dapper, balding little man in an expensive suit sat at a dark, wooden table. The whole room was filled with books and old-fashioned furniture, and in one corner a stereo played the violin-piano type music. It was all very nice and peaceful. The man had a number of small containers in front of him, and a teaspoon in one hand. By his elbow were a notepad and a pen. He looked up and caught sight of the three heads peeking around the door.

'Gracious, hello!' he said, in a posh voice. 'What brings you to my little hideout?'

Gaz glanced at the other two. This guy didn't look too dangerous. Straightening up, he strode into the room.

'We're here for my brother,' he said. 'We're looking for Molars – the Head of Security. Do you know where we can find him?'

'I'm afraid I don't know anyone by the name of Molars,' the man replied. 'I don't mix much with the security people. We get few visitors to this part of the building. I'm left to myself most of the time.'

Gaz was closer to the table now, and he couldn't

resist arching his neck to try and see what was in the containers. There was a range of things; a jar of frog-spawn, a tin of shoe polish, bowls of maggots, engine oil, and even a cup full of fish eyes. They watched as the man dipped his spoon into a bowl of raw eggs and raised it to his mouth, sniffing it delicately. The children stared, unable to take their eyes off the contents of that spoon. The man glanced up at them, a knowing smile on his face. He took another sniff. He made a note on the paper. Then he lifted the spoon to his mouth.

'You're not going to–' Gaz started.

'You wouldn't–' Hayley gulped.

'Eyuuugh–' Damo gasped.

The man put the spoon to his lips, and sucked the contents into the back of his throat. He swilled the bit of raw egg around his mouth, and then spat it out into a bucket that was sitting by his feet. Damo belched and covered his mouth, his cheeks bulging. Hayley went green. Gaz stuck his tongue out and gagged.

'What the hell are you doing?' he gasped, his face twisted up in disgust.

'It's not the most pleasant job in the world, I'll grant you,' the man said. 'But I'm good at it, you understand? It's what I do best. I'm the company's Disgustinger. I find the worst tastes imaginable and we mass-produce them. Then our agents sneak into farms and supermarkets all over the country and inject them into natural food. I make healthy food taste disgusting.'

'I knew it!' Damo exclaimed. 'I *knew* boiled cabbage didn't taste right. I've been telling my momma that for years!'

'Cabbage was one of my personal triumphs,' the Disgustinger smiled bashfully. 'It used to taste like potato crisps before I got my hands on it. And you know liver? That naturally tastes like southern-fried chicken. I soon changed that. But my personal best was spinach – spinach used to taste like mint chocolate mousse before we added our extract of sweaty Wellington boot. I'm particularly proud of spinach.'

'But why?' Hayley asked, twisting her hair. 'Why make good food taste like wellies?'

'Oh, so we can sell people the food *we* want them to eat,' the man told them, with a hint of pride in his voice. 'And we make it taste especially good. All of our ingredients are artificial … for maximum pleasure. Haven't you noticed how no child in this country wants to eat natural food any more? That's how good I am at my job.'

Gaz burped, and breathing into his hand, he grimaced.

'These *burps* are starting to smell now,' he said. 'What is it about this place that everything stinks so much?'

'Everything here smells …' the man smiled. 'Unless it's made *not* to smell. Here try this …'

He took out a little canister, and sprayed

something into his mouth. Then he offered it to Gaz.

'It takes away the odour. I need it for my work, you understand. Press down, and take a breath.'

Gaz took it tentatively, and sniffed it. Then he sprayed some in his mouth, breathing in as he did. He belched into his hand, and his face brightened.

'Hey, that's quite cool,' he said.

'Let me smell,' Hayley piped up, coming over to him.

He belched in her face.

'Yeah, that's nice,' she nodded. 'Like strawberries and vanilla.'

'Hey, give me a blast o' that!' Damo shuffled up to them.

He and Hayley each took a spray of the breath freshener.

'I could do with some of this stuff for my socks,' Damo grinned.

'The Security Office is on the top floor,' the Disgustinger informed them. 'The elevator is out the door, turn right, down the corridor, up the stairs and past the kitchens. Steer clear of the cooks – they're frightful creatures. I wish you luck in finding your friend.'

He picked up his spoon. Eager to avoid watching him take another mouthful, the children thanked him and made for the door. As they left, they heard a slurping sound behind them, and then the sound of raw egg being spat into a bucket.

6

The Kitchen Of Death

The flight of stairs led up to a landing, where there was another door. The steps started again beyond the door, but something made the Root Street Gang stop when they reached the top of the stairs. A small cuddly toy – a dog – was lying on its back near the top of the first flight of stairs. It seemed to have fallen down the steps, and its legs were waving around, but it couldn't get up. It was obviously robotic. The boys looked around warily, suspecting some kind of trap. Hayley picked it up and set it back on the floor of the landing.

The little dog immediately started towards the stairs again, but it was clear it would never make it down the steps on its own. Hayley grabbed it, and held onto it, tickling its tummy.

'Little mutt must be from in here,' Damo pointed towards the door. 'Check it out.'

A sign on the door read; 'Cybercritters: Taste-Test Units'.

The door stood ajar, and they gently pushed it open. The enormous, tiled room was full of metal shelves, and on every shelf were lines and lines of cuddly toys; everything from puppies to teddy bears, from kittens to rabbits. There were

thousands of them. Many of them were eating out of tiny troughs, or drinking from glass tubes.

Every now and again, one of the cybercritters would stop, squat and squeeze out a robo-pooh.

'Never seen a robot that could pooh before,' Gaz muttered. 'These things must be testing all that weird food they make here. Suppose what goes in must come out, yeah?'

'This place is totally twisted,' Damo muttered, waving a finger around the side of his head. 'I wanna split this scene. I'm getting really freaked out here.'

'Not without Joey,' Gaz replied.

'I think this one was trying to escape,' Hayley stroked the head of the robot she was carrying. 'I can feel its sadness – I mean, just look at its aura! I want to bring him with us. I'm going to call him Squirt.'

'What makes you think it's, like … y'know, a boy?' Damo sneered.

Hayley showed him.

'Oh,' Damo raised his eyebrows. 'I didn't know they put those on robots.'

'Okay,' said Gaz, who thought the idea of having their own robot was quite cool, even if it would need to be toilet-trained. 'But let's go. I'm getting really worried about Joey now. These are weird people we're dealing with here. Anybody who gives poison to cuddly toys just isn't right in the head. God knows what they're doing to poor Joey.'

They left the room and continued on up the stairs, being careful not to make any noise. Just before they reached the top, Gaz waved at them to drop down, and then ducked his head below the level of the top step. The others crawled up beside him and lifted their heads carefully to see over the top. At the end of the corridor were the doors of the elevator that would take them to the third floor. But before they reached it, they would have to get past the door to the kitchen, which was on the left side of the corridor. They could hear things moving around inside, and pots and cutlery clattering.

There were stainless steel cupboards and kitchen units against the walls of the corridor. Gaz got to his feet and darted to the nearest one, crouching down to hide behind the side of it. Damo scurried down to huddle beside him. Before Hayley could join them, somebody came out of the kitchen door, and the two boys squeezed back against the wall, desperately hoping they wouldn't be spotted. They couldn't see whoever it was, but it sounded like the person was wearing really high heels. Their footsteps were hard and sharp, and the person moved with small, short, quick steps.

The boys glanced back at Hayley ... and their gazes locked on her glowing pink face as they saw the terror in her eyes. Her head was raised just above the level of the stairs, and she was staring straight down the corridor. Her eyes were wide with horror.

'What hhhhave we … ahuh, ahuh … got hhhere?' a clicking voice demanded.

The boys' heads turned, and they found themselves looking into two huge, round, segmented eyes, set in a dark brown head topped with a pair of antennae and armed with heavy, pincer-like jaws. It was an enormous cockroach, and it was wearing a chef's uniform, complete with tall white hat. The boys burst out into long, high-pitched screams.

They tried to run, but the cockroach seized them with its clawed hands and dragged them into the kitchen. It was bustling with activity, the whole place filled with the giant insects. The smells told the two boys that this was no ordinary kitchen. Whatever they were cooking up here, it definitely wasn't dinner.

'Why are you putting ruddy *rattlesnake* venom in there, when I specifically told you to add two drops of ruddy *cobra* venom?' a chef was snapping at one of the younger cooks. 'Did you see me put any rattlesnake venom in there?'

'No, Chef,' the younger cockroach said, lowering his head in shame.

'Then why did you do it?'

'Don't know, Chef.'

'I catch you putting rattlesnake venom in that mix again, I'll have you back on toilet bowl duty so fast, your ruddy feet won't touch the ground, you got it?' the head chef growled, his jaws clicking as he talked.

'Yes, Chef.'

The head chef moved on, sniffing the vapour from another pot, growling orders and insulting his cowering assistants.

'Add some turpentine to this ... and some more bleach. It smells like my mother's feet. I like it!'

Then he noticed the other chef come in with the two boys.

'What you got there, Harold?'

'Two little ... ahuh, ahuh ... spiiiies, I think, Albert,' Harold replied.

'Spies, eh?' Albert leaned in close to study the trembling children. 'Trying to steal our recipes, are

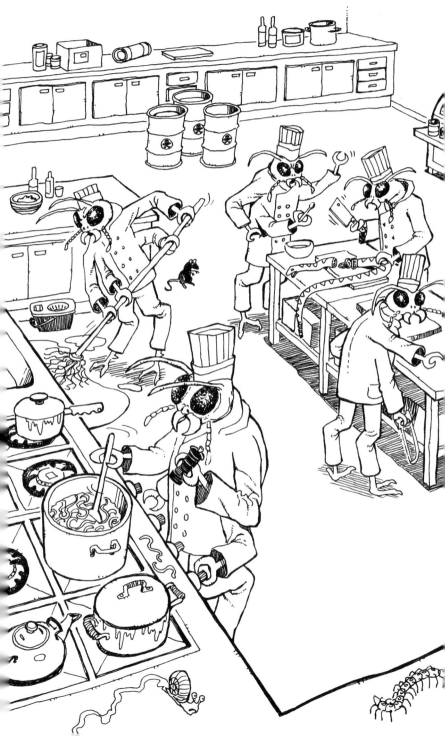

you? There's people who would pay a handsome price for my Lung Rotter Sauce, or my Stomach Bomb Stew. Who are you working for, eh? What's your game?'

'We're not w…w…working for anybody!' Gaz stammered. 'We're just looking for my little brother. He came in here looking for our f…f…football.'

'So! The old lost football story!' Albert's jaws clicked aggressively. 'If I had a cyanide tablet for every time I heard that old chestnut, I could retire early! Well, if you won't talk, we'll make you talk! Harold, bring me the Truth Scorpions.'

Harold took a jar down from a shelf and unscrewed the top. Reaching into it, he drew two large scorpions out by their tails. He handed them to Albert.

'One jab from this,' Albert clicked at the two boys, brandishing one of the twitching animals, 'and you'll tell me anything I want to know.'

'We'll tell you anything *anyway*!' Damo wailed. 'You don't need to use any flippin' scorpions!'

But the cockroach chef pulled the collar of his hoodie out and dropped the scorpion down the back of his neck. Damo howled, and then thrashed around. He stopped sud-denly, and his head tilted slowly to one side.

'Ow,' he moaned, dreamily.

'Hold this one, he's wriggling like a ruddy maggot!' Albert cried as Gaz fought to get away.

Two other cockroaches grabbed him, and the second scorpion was dropped down the back of his t-shirt. He pulled frantically at the claws of his captors, but it was no good. He felt the scorpion crawling around on his back, and then something sharp dug into his shoulder, and the whole world went a fluffy pink. Gaz felt himself overcome with an urge to tell everybody what he was thinking.

'Damo, I gotta tell ya, man,' he burped. 'I'm goin'

to wet myself if I don't get to a bog soon.'

'I know what you mean, dude,' Damo replied in a slurred voice. 'I'm havin' a problem holdin' it in meself. We need to get out of here, and find a john.'

'Enough!' Albert glared down at Gaz. 'Talk! Spill your secrets!'

Gaz tried to hold his breath, but it didn't work.

'I take Joey's teddy bear to bed with me sometimes!' he blurted out.

'I play with my sister's dolls!' Damo shouted, helplessly.

'I pretend my Action Man's married to Hayley's Barbie doll,' Gaz sobbed. 'I make them kiss!'

Damo laughed and cried at the same time.

'I love you, Gaz. You're my best pal.'

'You're my best mate too,' Gaz insisted. 'You've *always* been my best mate.'

'Stop this!' Albert snapped. 'Have you lost your minds? Stop this nonsense and confess your disgusting deeds!'

'I used to pick used chewing gum off the ground and eat it,' Damo whimpered.

'That's it!' Albert roared, his jaws clicking furiously. 'I've had enough of this! Harold, fetch down the big pot. We're going to cook up some human casserole!'

The boys were hauled over onto a counter, and held down while half a dozen cockroach chefs lifted a huge pot onto a nearby cooker. They took out some razor sharp knives and started to cut up some carrots and potatoes. The Truth Scorpions' venom was starting to wear off, and the fear began to set in again. Gaz and Damo screamed and struggled against their captors, but the giant insects were too strong.

'Noooo!' Damo shrieked, with tears in his eyes, as he was carried towards the big pot.

Suddenly, the door to the corridor burst open, and a flood of robotic, cuddly toys surged into the room in a wave of fake fur. Hundreds of them spread out along the floor and clambered up onto the tables and counters.

'SSSomebody's ssssset the cybercritters loose!' Harold squealed. 'Catch them, quick!'

This was easier said than done. Wherever the cockroaches stepped, their sharp, clawed feet got stuck in the backs of the cuddly robots. Free from the grip of their captors, Gaz and Damo watched, bemused, as the insect chefs scurried around, clumsily trying to round up the horde of soft toys. Some of the cybercritters were squirting out their dinners, and the floor quickly became slippery with the slick mess. Hayley appeared as if by magic beside the two boys, clutching Squirt in her arms.

'Come on!' she urged them. 'Run for it!'

They jumped down off the counter and waded through the furry tide to the door. Behind them, there came a screech of fury.

'Yooouuu're nnnot going anywhere!' Harold snarled at them.

The raging cockroach charged at them, but his clawed feet impaled a couple of mechanical rabbits, and then he skidded through a pool of robo-pooh and flipped onto his back. His feet flew into the air, throwing the unlucky bunnies far across the room.

The three children belted out of the kitchen, and down the corridor. Gaz slapped the button to call the elevator. It pinged gently. Behind them, Albert clawed his way out of the kitchen through the mass of robotic toys. Glaring at the children, he snarled, and clattered towards them.

'Come on! Come on!' Damo was yelling at the elevator doors.

There was another bell chime and the doors slid open. Gaz pushed the others in and punched the button to shut the doors again. They clamped closed just as Albert slammed into them with a frustrated roar.

They all slumped against the walls, exhausted. Gaz pulled out the bottom of his t-shirt, and the Truth Scorpion dropped to the floor. He kicked it away from him. Damo was struggling to find his scorpion in his big, baggy tracksuit top.

'Here, what are you doing?' Hayley asked. 'Let me help.'

She reached up the back of the jumper and was pulling the scorpion out when it twisted in her hand and stung her. Her face went all rosy, and her eyes glazed over.

'Aw, no,' Gaz groaned.

'Listen, I *have* to tell you this lads!' Hayley exclaimed, grinning madly. 'You've both been sending me Valentine cards for years!'

'No I haven't!' Damo snorted a little too loudly, rolling his eyes. 'Girls are so soppy.'

'Yeah!' Gaz spluttered. 'She's … she's lost her mind or somethin'. I never sent any cards …'

Both boys fell into an embarrassed silence, desperately hoping Hayley's scorpion sting would wear off quickly.

7

Dying To Go

The elevator took Gaz, Hayley and Damo up to the top floor. In the few seconds of peace, they each treated themselves to a sweet from the bag, as a reward for escaping from the cockroaches, and to help Hayley get over her embarrassing bout of honesty.

'We'd better go easy on these,' Gaz said, warily. 'There's not many left. We've got to have some for Molars.'

When the doors slid open, they found themselves on a flat, open section of rooftop. Across from them was a door, marked 'Management'. It was the only door they could see.

'So where's the security office?' Damo moaned. 'How do we find Joey?'

'I don't know,' Gaz sighed. 'But I need to go for a pee right now, or I'm goin' to burst.'

'Me too,' Damo agreed.

They went up to the base of a chimney that jutted out from the roof, and unzipped their flies.

'Bet I can get higher up than you can,' Gaz said.

'In your dreams, bud!' Damo laughed.

'Typical boys!' Hayley muttered, disgusted.

She turned away to look out over the rooftops. She needed to go too, but she decided to hold on until she found a proper toilet. When the boys were done, all three of them walked across to the door marked 'Management'. Gaz knocked nervously, and a voice inside beckoned them in. They opened the door to find themselves faced with a small science lab, and a wall of monitors that showed lots of different views of the factory. A thin, angular man wearing a white coat sat with his back to them on a stool at the large desk. He was working with some test tubes. He swivelled to face them, his skinny legs folded at sharp angles. They recognised his exhausted-looking face immediately. It was Cornelius, the man they had met when they had first entered the factory.

'Ah,' he said. 'You made it. Have you got the sweets?'

The three children looked at each other, mystified. Gaz handed over the bag. Cornelius stood up and took it, hefting in his hand and looking inside.

'My! We *were* hungry, weren't we? Ahhh, nobody can resist the smell of my jellies. One of my best inventions,' he chuckled. 'Been doing any burping, lately?'

Hayley couldn't contain herself any longer.

'Can I use your loo?' she asked, biting her thumbnail.

'What's going on?' Gaz demanded.

'You've just joined my little club,' Cornelius waved his hand towards the monitors. 'Let me introduce myself fully; my name is Cornelius … Cornelius *Byle*. I own this factory.'

'Then you are one twisted biscuit,' Damo blurted out at him.

'Where's your loo?' Hayley bounced up and down on the balls of her feet, her hands clutching Squirt a little too tightly.

'I may be one twisted biscuit,' Byle smiled. 'But

tomorrow, I will *still* be a twisted biscuit … and you will all be *dead*. You've each had more than enough of these sweets to make sure that you are well and truly doomed.'

'What do you mean?' the three of them all chimed at once.

'The sweets were poisoned,' Byle grinned. 'In a matter of hours, you will all shrivel up like raisins and die.'

The three children went deathly pale.

'Fortunately,' he raised one finger. 'I have an antidote–'

He held up his hands as the children started shouting. They fell silent.

'To get the antidote for yourselves,' he went on. 'You have to do something for me. I want you to bring all your friends to this factory. My zombies are constantly falling apart, which means I'm always having to make new ones. It's a complex chemical process, and I don't get many volunteers. A dozen or so of your friends would do.'

'You're off your head,' Gaz gasped.

'Not at all,' Byle shook his head. 'It's just business. I have a company to run, and it's so hard to get good staff these days. Bring back some of your friends so I can make them into zombies, and you three will get your antidote.'

'I NEED TO GO TO THE LOO RIGHT NOW!' Hayley shrieked, her legs crossed.

'Oh,' Byle frowned. 'The bathroom's that door to your left.'

Hayley rushed over to the door, and yanked it open, hurrying inside. She closed the door, and the boys looked awkwardly at each other. They weren't sure what to do.

'Well?' Byle asked. 'Do you want the antidote or not?'

'We need to wait for Hayley,' Gaz gulped.

He really didn't want to see his friends turned into zombies. But he didn't want to shrivel up and die like a raisin either. They all stood quietly for a couple of minutes, the boys turning to gaze at all the lab equipment that filled the room.

The door opened and Hayley came out.

'It's really posh in there,' she said. 'There's gold taps and everything.'

'You didn't flush,' Byle said, sourly.

'Sorry,' Hayley muttered.

She went back inside, and there came the sound of the toilet flushing ... And then a mighty explosion rocked the room – smoke and flames burst from the bathroom and the plaster was shaken from the walls as they were all knocked off their feet. Hayley staggered out, her hands over her ears. Squirt waddled out after her and fell over, dazed.

'I just flushed the toilet,' she said in a shocked, timid voice. 'And it *blew up.*'

The boys were stunned. Byle got slowly to his feet, one hand on his head as he tried to keep his balance.

'What ...' he started to say, but had to stop as he got dizzy. He tried again. 'What else have you

eaten today? Tell me what you did in the factory. I need to know everything!'

The children looked at each other, but since they were all going to die like raisins, it didn't make any difference anyway. Gaz told Byle everything – about being chased by the zombies, about riding the conveyor belt over the tanks of weird stuff, about meeting the Disgustinger and setting the cybercritters free, and about escaping from the cockroach chefs.

'So let me get this straight,' Byle strode over to a white board on the wall, and started writing strange chemical symbols on it. 'You let your skin get soaked by the zombie disinfectant, you inhaled the Disgustinger's breath freshener, you were injected with the venom of Truth Scorpions, *and* you ate my sweets?'

'Yeah,' all three kids said at once.

Byle finished writing out his calculations, and stood back, his hands shaking. He turned to glare at them, his loosely-rooted teeth rattling in his skull.

'That's an impossible combination of chemicals,' he whispered, trembling. 'You should be dead. But since you're not dead, and since my toilet just blew up, I can come to only one conclusion. You are all filled to the brim with highly explosive urine.'

'What d'ya mean?' Damo asked.

'He means our pee can explode,' Gaz translated, as a nasty plan started to form in his mind.

'You could go off at any second,' Byle whimpered. 'Don't … don't make any sudden moves.'

'I don't know,' Gaz smiled slightly, his fear making him angry again.

'If we don't get that antidote, I might lose the rag a bit – and I can go a bit mental when I'm really angry. I might start jumpin' around ... and I'm burstin' to go. I might go right here on your chair!'

'NO!' Byle cried.

Hayley and Damo stared at Gaz. Was he serious?

'Really, I'd do it – I'd do it right now,' Gaz nodded, his jaw jutting out.

'Me too,' Damo added suddenly. 'And I might just do some hip-hop dancing on your desk! I can spin around on my hands!'

'I can do gymnastics,' Hayley piped up. 'Want to see my back-flip?'

They all climbed up onto the desk.

'Right,' Gaz called out. 'On the count of three, we let rip! One ... Two ...'

'Please, please don't!' Byle sobbed. 'I'll give you the antidote. Just don't do anything stupid!'

He pulled a little bottle from his coat pocket and handed it to Gaz.

'Oh, and we want my little brother back too,' Gaz

demanded.

'I never took him!' Byle whined. 'He's still out in the yard. He was hiding there the whole time.'

He pointed to a monitor, and sure enough, there was Joey, peeping out from behind a stack of barrels.

'That little weed,' Gaz growled, turning to the other two. 'I *told* you he was good at screaming.'

* * *

After knocking back the antidote to the poison, Gaz, Hayley and Damo made their way extremely cautiously down to the yard. It was all very well being able to scare Cornelius Byle into giving them the antidote, but there was still no telling whether or not they might explode. They walked down the last flight of stairs very slowly and gently. Taking small, timid steps, they shuffled out into the yard.

'Where were you?' Joey exclaimed, coming out of his hiding place, holding their football. 'I saw you go inside, and then you were gone for ages. I was going to go home and tell Mam!'

Gaz leaned over him, his hands clenched into fists.

'I've a good mind to kick your–'

'Ah, leave him alone,' Damo said. 'He caught us out – we should respect the little dude. You don't want to go starting a fight, Gaz. Not with what's in your bladder. Come on – let's go home.'

But Gaz was determined to get revenge. Grabbing his brother's shoulder, he swung back his leg and delivered a sound kick to Joey's backside. Just as he did, there was a deafening crack, and a deep rumble. At first, the others covered their heads, sure that Gaz was exploding right in front of them. But he was still standing there when they opened their eyes, and the rumbling noise was getting louder. He was looking up. They looked up too.

A tall chimney was toppling over towards them, its shadow falling over them, the huge tower of concrete plummeting straight down at them. There was no time to do anything but close their eyes and wait to be crushed. It crashed to the ground just short of them, smashing at their feet, sending shards of concrete and dust flying in all directions. Hayley gave Gaz and Damo a disgusted look.

'Was that the chimney we …?' Damo began.

'Yeah,' Gaz nodded. 'We'd better go. Quick.'

'Do you think the antidote will fix the whole exploding pee thing?' Hayley wondered aloud as the Root Street Gang walked towards the hole under the back wall.

'Hope so,' Gaz grunted. He put his arm around Joey's shoulders, glad that his little brother was all right after all. 'If it doesn't, we'll be going to the toilet very, very carefully for the rest of our lives.'

OISÍN McGANN has also written *The Evil Hairdo*, another in the 'Forbidden Files' series. He is the author of five Flyers: *Mad Grandad's Flying Saucer*; *Mad Grandad's Robot Garden*; *Mad Grandad and the Mutant River*; *Mad Grandad and the Kleptoes*, *Mad Grandad's Wicked Pictures* and a number of acclaimed novels for older readers: *The Gods and Their Machines*; *The Harvest Tide Project*; *Under Fragile Stone*, *Small-Minded Giants* and *Ancient Appetites*.

If you enjoyed the adventures of The Root Street Gang, you'll love Melanie's story in The Evil Hairdo. Turn the page to read a chapter ...

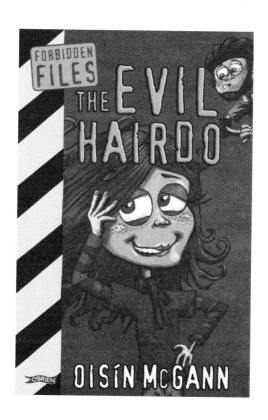

I Should Be On MTV
Or Something

I ran down the street and across the main road to the new salon. I took a long, long look at the poster in the window, buzzing with excitement, and then I pushed the door open.

The place was like something out of Mum's magazines. It wasn't that big, but it was really stylish, with huge mirrors, and everything was in wood and metal and curved plastic. There was one chair, which looked like it belonged on television. It had black leather and steel handles for raising and lowering and turning it. There were bottles of *Witch-Craft* shampoo and conditioner and other stuff laid neatly on shelves. And in frames on the walls there were posters of the girls from the band, looking like goddesses in the hippest gear.

'What a beautiful little girl!' a voice purred, making me look towards the back of the shop.

There by a door stood a woman who seemed made of wood and plastic and leather herself. She was lovely, but very thin, and very, very pale. She had white skin, light blonde hair and pale green eyes. The leather trousers, the black silk shirt with very big cuffs and the fabulously pointy shoes (also black) made her look even paler and thinner. I fingered the coins in my pocket and looked around me, suddenly feeling a bit awkward.

'And what can I do for you, young miss?' she asked, gazing right into my eyes.

'I ... I'd like the, y'know ... the ...' I couldn't seem to get the words out.

'You'd like the *WitchCraft* hair,' she finished for me.

'Yes,' I hung my head, feeling a bit silly about being shy. I'm not normally a shy person.

'Take a seat.' The pale lady waved towards the chair. 'My name is Gail ... and I am your stylist.'

A shiver ran down my back as she said that. I'd never had a *stylist* before. Mum always took me to the hairdressers. And now I was in an Official *Witch-Craft* Salon! This was just *so* cool! I climbed up on the chair and Gail tied up that smock they use to keep the hair off your clothes. She raised the chair so I could see myself in the mirror.

'Let us begin,' she cried, as she spun the chair around and gently tilted my head back over the sink.

I closed my eyes while she washed my hair, but it didn't feel like a normal hair wash. First it fizzed, then it itched, then she rinsed it off and washed it again. This time it felt a bit like there were worms in my hair and I was starting to get a bit scared. But just before I started to cry, she rubbed my hair in a towel and moved me so I faced the mirror. My hair was a tangled mess, but even though it was wet, I could see that instead of my usual brown, it was black with a green tinge to it. My heart gave a little flutter.

'I shouldn't really tell you this,' Gail whispered, as she leaned close to my ear. 'But before they became big and famous, *WitchCraft* were just cool, good-looking girls like you. They were smart though.

They knew that when you've got all the right gear, and you've got the right look, you're already on your way to being a superstar! So let's see if we can make a star out of *you*!'

I giggled like a little kid and nodded excitedly.

She carefully combed my hair out and parted it. Then she took her scissors from a plastic jar on the counter. Once the scissors started moving, they did not stop. Even when she held them away from my head, they kept clicking as if they had a life of their own. Then they would swoop back in again like an attacking bird and I would hear them close to my ears, nipping hair and tapping against the comb. This went on for some time before the clicking suddenly stopped. She washed my hair again and then she picked up the hairdryer. When she had finished drying and had brushed away the stray hairs, Gail stepped back.

'Well, what do you think?' she said, holding up a mirror and showing me the back.

'Wow,' was all I could manage.

She had done it. I had *WitchCraft* hair.

'Wow,' I said again. I touched it just to be sure it was mine. It was.

'Your hair was perfect for the style,' she smiled. 'I was really able to give some *life* to this one. I think you look gorgeous. You should be on MTV.'

I grinned giddily. Handing her the money, I thanked her and ran out of the salon. I was just *dying* to show my friends.

As I hurried away, I glanced back once and saw Gail watching me. She had a funny look on her face – as if she had won a game or something. And she was staring at me. I didn't give it much thought at the time. I was too happy to notice anything was wrong.

* * *

The Evil Hairdo by Oisín McGann, 2006
ISBN: 978-0-86278-940-4
Available in all good bookshops

Also in the Forbidden Files Series

The Book of Curses

By Conor Kostick, illustrated by Julie Parker

Alex Zwick is a stubborn, **bold** boy. So when he gets his hands on a **magic** book, he won't stop making wishes, even when they go **horribly** wrong. Can Alex and his friend Emily outsmart the book? Or will the chillingly **evil** laughter of the book yet again ring out in triumph?

The Witch Apprentice
By Marian Broderick, illustrated by Francesca Carabelli

There's something **very** odd going on in Anna Kelly's new home – her guardians, Grizz and Wormella Mint, are **witches**, and they want Anna to help them with their nasty spells! So Anna's stuck in their horrible house, chopping up **toadstools** and scrambling **frogspawn**, with no one but Charlie the cat for company. Is there **any** way out for her? But then she finds an **evil, old spell book** in the cellar – can Anna make the magic work for **her?**